ORP GOES TO THE HOOP

SUZY KLINE is the author of the popular *Herbie Jones* books. In addition to writing, she teaches elementary school in Torrington, Connecticut, where she lives with her husband, two daughters, and three cats. *Orp Goes to the Hoop* is her third book about Orville Rudemeyer Pygenski, Jr., the hero of *Orp* and *Orp and the Chop Suey Burgers.*

Avon Books are available at special quantity discounts for bulk purchases for sales promotions, premiums, fund raising or educational use. Special books, or book excerpts, can also be created to fit specific needs.

For details write or telephone the office of the Director of Special Markets, Avon Books, Dept. FP, 1350 Avenue of the Americas, New York, New York 10019, 1-800-238-0658.

ORP GOES TO THE HOOP

SUZY KLINE

AN AVON CAMELOT BOOK

ACKNOWLEDGMENTS

Special appreciation goes to the University of Connecticut Husky basketball team and their "Dream Season of 1989," to Scott Burrell's pass and Tate George's one-second shot. And to Husky Murray Williams, who came to my classroom. Thank you all for your inspiration.

AVON BOOKS
A division of
The Hearst Corporation
1350 Avenue of the Americas
New York, New York 10019

First Avon Camelot Printing: February 1993

CAMELOT TRADEMARK REG. U.S. PAT. OFF. AND IN OTHER COUNTRIES, MARCA REGISTRADA, HECHO EN U.S.A.

Printed in the U.S.A.

OPM   10   9   8   7   6   5   4   3   2   1

*Dedicated with love to the
basketball players in my family:*

*My father, Harry C. Weaver, forward
Fairmount High School, Indiana
Basketball Scholarship to Wabash College, 1928*

*My mother, Martha Swihart Weaver, forward
South Whitley High School, Indiana
High Point girl, 1928*

*My daughter, Jennifer Kline, center and captain
Torrington High School, Connecticut
Scholar Athlete Award, 1988*

Contents

CHAPTER ONE

To Play or Not to Play?

"ORVIE!" My sister hollered into the bathroom. "You've been in there an hour now!"

Of course I was. I get my best ideas when I'm sitting in the tub. The window was locked shut. It had to be one of the coldest days in Connecticut. And with the old radiator we have in the bathroom, it can get nippy. Thomas Jefferson had his great house called Monticello. I call our place Montichillo.

I was sitting in the tub wearing my Cornell Middle School jacket, relaxing, and brainstorming things to do in winter.

1. downhill skiing
2. luge
3. snowshoeing
4. ice hockey
5. ice skating
6. ice fishing
7. basketball

Basketball. My friend Derrick asked me if I wanted to try out for the team. I was still thinking about it. My dad was a pretty good player. We have pictures of his high school and college teams in the dining room. He even got an award for being the scholar-athlete at his high school. Most of the basketballs in our attic are half filled with air. Usually Derrick and I put them on our heads when we feel like being silly. I haven't bothered to fill them up and use them. There's even a hoop in the garage but it has to be put up.

Baseball is my game. I can't wait for spring practice. The coach said I had the fastest pitch in Little League and this year I get to be Cornell Middle School's starting pitcher. I'd better stick to one sport.

Suddenly, the bathroom door swung open. My sister, Chloe, who is in fifth grade, quickly cov-cred her eyes. "Ooops!" she said. "I just meant to bang on the door."

I could tell she wanted to floss her teeth. She had her dental floss in her hand.

"Do what you have to do," I said, adding number eight to my winter activities.

8. Throwing snowballs in my sister's face

Chloe peaked through her fingers. "ORVIE! You're just sitting in the bathtub again with your clothes on! Get out!"

I decided not to make a fuss. Besides, the phone was ringing. Derrick said he'd call after school about something important.

As I walked into the kitchen, Mom handed me the phone. "It's for you," she said.

"Thanks." I took the phone cord into the living room and plopped down on the couch. "Hello?" I said.

"Big news, Orp!"

"What's up, Derrick?"

"Basketball tryouts start tonight. Have you decided yet if you're going out for the team?"

"I don't think so. I've never been on a basketball team before." I decided not to mention how great I was at the Fisher Price Basketball Set when I was four.

"Well, now that you are a seventh grader you have a chance to try out for one."

"How come you're interested? You don't like to play sports."

"Ellen Fairchild is a cheerleader. She's going to be rooting at all the games and riding on the team bus."

I knew it!

I put my long legs up on the back of the couch. Derrick's whole life revolved around Ellen Fairchild. Saturdays, he volunteered to work at her uncle's pet shop where she worked. Now he was going to join a basketball team?

"Think you have a chance to make the team?" I asked.

"I'm already on it."

"What?" I sat up right away. I was shocked!

"I'm the team statistician. I keep track of each player's shots, rebounds, stolen balls, everything. Coach Casey is a neat guy. Anyway, there's try-outs tonight at 6 P.M. in the gym. Why don't you try out and we can ride on the team bus together?"

I could picture it. Ellen, Derrick and me on a seat. It didn't seem very exciting. Just then Chloe came in and turned on the TV set with a pair of needlenose pliers. (Our TV knob has been broken for almost a year now.)

"Excuse me, Derrick," I cupped the phone. "Would you mind, Chloe. This is a private call."

"Yes, I DO mind. This living room is not private. It's public. It belongs to our family."

Sisters. I was glad I had just one. Slowly, I picked up the phone and returned to the bathtub. It was the only really private place in the house since the cord didn't reach my bedroom.

"You still there?" I said.

"Are you going to play basketball or not?" Derrick was there.

"I don't know. I've watched a lot of games on TV and some seventh and eighth-grade teams last year at school, but I've never really played."

"Your dad did. Maybe basketball talent is passed through the genes."

"Or the Levis," I suggested.

Derrick cracked up.

Just then Mom called from the kitchen, "ORVIE! COME AND SET THE TABLE FOR DINNER, AND SLICE THE ONIONS."

Suddenly I had a new motivation. "Okay, Derrick, I'll meet you at the gym in five minutes."

As I returned the phone to the kitchen, I said, "Mom, I have to go down to the school gym for an hour or so . . ."

"What for?"

All I had to say was those two magical words . . .

"Extracurricular activities." Mom was real neat

5

about letting me get out of chores when I had something to do for school.

"What kind of extracurricular activities?"

I wondered if I should tell her. Mom can get very excited about things.

"I'm THINKING about going out for the basketball team."

Mom stopped slicing a tomato. "Really?"

"Yeah."

"How exciting! Did you know I played on the girls' varsity team in high school?"

The thought of my mother dribbling a basketball down the court never occurred to me. It was hard to picture.

"No kidding, Mom?"

"I was team captain. I hardly missed any of my free throws." Then she stepped back and shot a tomato into the salad bowl.

Suddenly I started thinking seriously about genes. Maybe Derrick was right. Geez, I thought. It's on BOTH sides of my family.

"Well, I'm leaving."

Now Mom held up a dill pickle and took four steps back. "Have fun!"

As I headed out the door, I heard the plunk and Mom exclaim, "Bull's eye!"

Basketball?

I'll give it a try.

CHAPTER TWO

Getting Hooked on Basketball

When I got to the gym, Derrick was dribbling the basketball around the court. It was pretty sad. He kept bouncing it on his foot. I was glad Derrick was good at math. He was definitely not good at sports.

"Hey, Orp!" Derrick said, tossing me the ball.

I caught it and smoothed my hands over the tiny bumps on the rubber. I liked the feel of it. It was good and firm. I bounced it a few times and walked over to the hoop.

I took my first shot.

Swish! It went in.

I took my second shot. That went in, too.

"I knew it!" Derrick laughed. "It's in the Levis! You're going to make the A team."

I held the ball next to my face. I even liked the smell of it. That was when I looked at my watch. It was 5:06 on November 12th. I wanted to remember the moment because that was when I started playing basketball.

For the next 45 minutes, I just kept shooting the ball and jumping high to get my own rebound. I loved playing. I didn't want to stop.

When I heard voices at the back of the gym, I turned around. Four eighth graders strolled in, each bouncing his own basketball. I remembered them from last year. They were on the starting five of the A team.

"Who's the hotshot?" a tall black kid said.

Derrick gave me an elbow. "Don't mess with him. He's the strongest guy on the team, Moses Miller."

I stopped bouncing the ball and let them have the court.

"You look pretty good, kid. What's your name?" another boy asked. "You a seventh grader?"

I nodded. "I'm Orp."

The boy shook my hand. "I'm Danny Chin. Orp is an unusual name."

"Yeah, I'm not crazy about it," I said. I didn't

think I needed to tell them that I started an I Hate My Name Club last summer. And that it lasted for just one meeting.

"I'm Moses. I'm not crazy about my name either."

I shook the black boy's hand.

"Want to play some one-on-one?" Moses asked.

"Sure," I said, not knowing exactly what that was.

He dribbled the ball around me like Michael Jordan on TV. Just when I moved to the left, he moved to the right and made a basket. "That's one," he said.

When he inbounded the ball again, I tried to stay with him, but his moves were too good. He dribbled right in for an easy lay-up. "That's two," he replied.

By the time he'd scored five baskets, lots of other guys had showed up and were shooting at the opposite hoop.

Bill Brown and Ike Farley, the other eighth graders, introduced themselves and joined us.

When the coach blew his whistle, we all gathered around. "TAKE FOUR LAPS!" he shouted.

Derrick sat down at the table and looked over his clipboard. Then he started doing a lot of writing.

I figured there were about 28 of us running around the court. Danny Chin was yards ahead of anyone else. Bill Brown ran next to me. "Coach Casey is tough, but he's fair. If you work hard, he'll respect you and give you playing time."

"How many make the A team?" I asked. "And what's the difference between the A team and the B team?"

"Last year, the coach put 12 guys on the A team and the rest on the B team. The A team plays games. The B team works on skills and sometimes a guy on the B team improves and moves up."

"I have to work on my moves," I said as we ran our second lap.

"I work on mine in my attic just like in that movie *Hoosiers*. The coach took the whole team to see it last year. I set chairs up and dribble around them. Mom tells me it's like living in an earthquake zone, but she lets me do it."

I laughed. I liked Bill Brown. His mom sounded like mine. Getting excited over little things. I also liked the movie. I saw *Hoosiers* twice with Uncle Gus.

When we took our fourth lap, one of the other seventh graders started to slow down and do a half jog, half walk.

Coach Casey took off his baseball cap, ran his fingers through his red hair, and then put his cap back on. "Hey, Monroe!"

Monroe, who was just walking now, waved to the coach.

"You can continue walking out to the locker room and out of the gym. Nobody walks when I say jog."

Monroe shrugged and left the gym.

I was shocked. The coach seemed really tough. But then I wondered. Did that Monroe guy really want to make the team? He didn't act like it.

After we ran four laps, the coach had us do some shooting, passing, dribbling and more running.

Ike Farley kept bragging about being high-point man last year and ranked on lots of the seventh graders. When I missed a free throw, he said, "The hotshot isn't so hot."

"Cut it out, Ike!" Moses said.

I gave Moses a smile. We had something in common. A name we didn't like.

At 6:30, the coach blew his whistle again. "See you guys tomorrow at 3:00 for final tryouts."

Derrick came rushing over to me. "You did really well, Orp! The coach asked me to keep track of lay-ups and free-throw shooting. You made 17 lay-ups and five free throws."

"I have to work on those," I said. "Maybe the custodian would let me come in early tomorrow morning."

Just as the boys were filing out, the cheerleading squad came down from the bleachers. It was their turn for the gym. Derrick made some excuse to me that he had to get home, and then he made a beeline for Ellen Fairchild. She waved at me. I waved back.

After I talked with the custodian, three cheerleaders came over and said hi. I wasn't used to that.

As I hopped on my bike and rode home, I wondered where I was going to practice my moves. It was getting dark.

Then I remembered what Bill Brown had said.

CHAPTER THREE

Basketball Takes on New Light

I went straight up to the attic and pumped some air into Dad's old basketballs. I arranged a few lawn chairs in the middle of the floor and started dribbling around them. It wasn't two minutes before Mom, Dad and Chloe showed up.

"What's going on up here?" Mom asked.

Then she saw for herself. "You're dribbling a ball on our ceiling?"

Dad made a quick suggestion. "Why don't you practice out in the garage driveway? I'll put up the hoop and some lights."

"You will?" I said.

"YOU WILL?" Mom asked. "I didn't realize you were handy like that, dear. I could add a few things to your list like our TV knob, our oven timer, our . . ."

"Priorities first!" Dad said with a smile. "My son wants to play some round ball. That's more important than any knob or timer."

Mom made a face. Then she looked at me. "So, you like to play, huh?"

I nodded.

"Well, grab a ham grinder on your way out. You have to eat something," Mom replied.

I wolfed one down as we went out to the garage. Then I held the ladder while Dad banged some nails and a few of his fingers. After he shouted a few choice words, he finally attached the old hoop. We got out a box of Christmas tree lights and started stringing them up around the door.

A few minutes later, Mom came outside with a glass of milk. I drank it right away. "Christmas decorations on the 12th of November?"

"The stores do it," Dad said. Then he put a big Santa Claus light in the corner of the garage.

"Now, son, what do you think you need to work on first?"

"Free throws and . . . moves. I got whipped today, Dad, in a one-on-one game."

"Moves, huh? Let's see . . ."

14

I watched my dad dribble down the driveway and dunk a lay-up shot.

"Gee, Dad! You're great!"

"Well, it's been a few years—like 25—but I can teach you a few basics." Then he paused. "I always hoped that you'd like basketball, Orvie, but I knew you were into baseball and I wanted you to follow your own interests, not mine."

"Do you think a good baseball pitcher can be a good basketball player, too?"

"Orv, the skills you've learned as a pitcher may just win a few games for your basketball team. Good throwing is a fundamental skill. You also know the importance of teamwork and team spirit."

While I was thinking about what Dad said, Mom took the ball away from him. I didn't even realize she was still standing there. "I can show you how to shoot free throws. That's a very fundamental skill in basketball too. In fact, many games are won by good free-throw shooting."

Dad took a step back and watched. His eyebrows were raised. I wondered if he knew about Mom's basketball career.

"It helps to establish a routine, Orvie. Try to do the same thing each time you go to the line. Put one foot slightly ahead of the other. Raise the ball with your right hand, sink your knees, rise up and push the ball away with your body."

Dad and I watched her as she positioned her feet in front of the hoop. Dad gave me this look which said, this should be good!

Mom took a breath. Then she bounced the ball three times, sank her knees, rose up and pushed the ball in a perfect arc aimed straight for the basket.

The ball hit the backboard and rolled around the rim a few times. Then it fell in the net.

I could tell Dad was impressed. He started clapping. "Way to go, Margie!"

Mom beamed. Then she handed the ball back to Dad. "I'll let you take over from here, dear."

Dad laughed.

That night Dad and I played ball for two hours. It was like getting a refresher course in math or something. He crammed every bit of information that he knew about the sport in my head.

That night, I made a list in my room.

1. Passing – good passes are essential. Shift your weight from your rear foot to your front foot. Target your receiver's chest.

2. Dribbling – learn how to do it with your left hand and right. Push the ball with your finger tips. Bounce the ball about waist level. Keep your chin up so you know where you're going.

3. Guarding - stay close to your man. Don't watch his shoulder or head - he can fake his moves. Watch his waist. Hustle and be aggressive. Stay between your man and the basket.

4. Shooting - be patient. Wait for the good shot. Work on your jump shot. Release the ball at the top of your jump. Keep your right elbow close to your body and shoot with your fingertips.

5. Free throws - Establish your own routine. Take a breath. Bounce the ball. Put one foot slightly ahead of the other. Raise the ball with your right hand, sink your knees, rise up, pushing the ball away.

When I got to number six, Chloe knocked on my door. "Yeah?" I said. I didn't appreciate being disturbed.

"May I come in?"

"I'm busy."

"For a minute. It's important."

What's important to my sister is usually not important to me. The last few times she barged in my room, she needed my opinion about a novel she was writing. Usually it's a dumb romance.

"Later," I said.

"Ellen Fairchild asked me to talk to you."

I put my pencil down and opened the door. "Ellen Fairchild? What's going on?"

"She just likes Derrick as a friend, and she doesn't want him to be her boyfriend."

I raised my eyebrows. Poor Derrick. Then I began to wonder what this had to do with me.

"She wants you to tell me what she should do."

Being a best friend had its responsibilities. I sat down on my bed and thought about it. I was thinking so hard I didn't even say anything about Chloe sitting next to me.

"I was going to give her some advice," Chloe said, "but she didn't ask for my opinion."

Finally, I looked at my sister. "Tell her to be honest. She shouldn't lead a guy on."

That was when Chloe gave me this funny look. "Gee, Orp, I didn't know you had it in you."

I returned to my desk. I wanted to go over my list again, go to bed, and get up early to practice my free-throw shooting. "Good-bye, Chloe," I said.

" 'Night, Orp."

Then she stopped halfway to the door. "If you become a basketball star, will you still say hi to me in the halls?"

I gave my sister this weird look. "What?" I tried to avoid her in the halls now.

"I just have this feeling that you are going to be

popular at Cornell Middle School and you might change your personality or something." Then her voice got real soft. "I like you the way you are now."

"Huh?"

I looked around. Who was she talking to? Not me. Not the pain that she complained to Mom about.

"Chloe, I don't even know if I'm going to make the B team. I just found out today that I love basketball like I do baseball. And . . . well, I'm excited. It's a great feeling."

Chloe leaned on my chair. "Did you know while you were practicing in the gym, four cheerleaders told me that they liked you?"

Four?

After I recovered from the initial shock, I thought about it. Could it be those three who came up to say hi? Who was the fourth?

"That includes . . ." Chloe said as she walked out the door, "Ellen Fairchild."

CHAPTER FOUR

Jenny Lee

Ellen Fairchild likes me? Derrick's Ellen Fairchild? This could be tricky.

Girls. I never thought about them much. Except, maybe Jenny Lee. I opened my drawer and pulled out her latest letter.

Jenny Lee was different from most girls.

For one thing, she was the only person who called me Orville. When she came to visit last summer with her mother and father (her mother and my mother were close friends in high school), we started an I Hate My Name Club. She didn't like her name because there were always three Jennifers in her class. Her seventh-grade class solved the problem this year by making one a Jennifer, one a Jen, and her a Jenny Lee.

Writing to her is kind of like having a girlfriend, but no one has to know about it. I like it like that. I don't have a lot of privacy in my life. Derrick thinks she's a pen pal. Chloe thinks she's just a good friend. I told Jenny Lee not to put any red hearts on the outside of the envelope.

But I said she could put as many as she wanted on the inside.

Just before I went to bed that night, I lay back on my pillow and read her letter for the fourth time. My dog, Ralph, was resting his head on my chest.

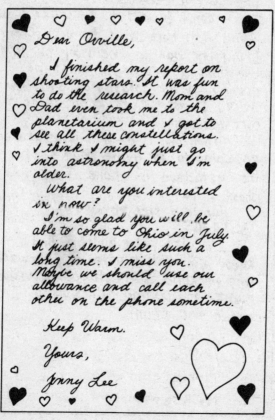

Dear Orville,

I finished my report on shooting stars. It was fun to do the research. Mom and Dad even took me to the planetarium and I got to see all these constellations. I think I might just go into astronomy when I'm older.

What are you interested in now?

I'm so glad you will be able to come to Ohio in July. It just seems like such a long time. I miss you. Maybe we should use our allowance and call each other on the phone sometime.

Keep Warm.

Yours,

Jenny Lee

I decided to write her a quick note before I went to bed.

Dear Jenny Lee,
    I think it's great you're into astronomy! I can send you a neat book about the stars that I got last Christmas.
    You asked about my new interest. It's BASKETBALL!
    I can't believe it. It's like I got stung with this wild tropical fever. I put the ball in the hoop the first two times I tried. It must be destiny. After that net swished twice, I wanted to keep doing it over and over.
    Tomorrow, I'm getting up at 6:00 and going to the gym. That's when the custodian is there. I want to shoot a few.
    Hundred free throws.
    Ha. Ha.
    I'm glad we're writing. And I know what I'll do with my allowance this weekend. I'll call you Saturday night at 7:00 and tell you if I made the team.

    Yours,
    Orville
P.S. You keep warm too.

When I turned off the light and rolled over, I felt Ralph's cold black nose next to my neck.

"Did you ever play basketball?" I asked. It seemed like everyone else in the family did.

But I fell asleep before I heard my dog's answer.

CHAPTER FIVE

An Early Bird

At 5:58, I left a note on the kitchen table for Mom.

Mom,
    I left early for school. See you after basketball tryouts.
            Love,
             Orvie
    P.S. I made myself a tuna sandwich, packed two apples and four oatmeal cookies. You know I'm a chef. I can take care of myself.

I jumped on my rusty bike, plopped my round ball, books and lunch in the basket and took off.

As I pedaled down the street, I spotted three birds singing on the branches of a red maple tree and nine chirping on the telephone wire. Morning is my favorite time of day. The sun was just coming up. Everything was still and beautiful.

I thought about Jenny Lee and her interest in astronomy. As I rounded the corner, I wondered what she would say the sunrise looked like.

A fried egg?

A marshmallow on hot chocolate?

Melting margarine?

As I parked my bike just outside the school gym, I knew what the sunrise looked like to me. A golden basketball. Then I reached for my own and dribbled it through the open door.

Mr. Beausoleil was sweeping the lobby. "Hey, Orp! You made it! When you asked me if you could come at 6:00 this morning, I thought you were joking."

"I have to work on some fundamentals, Mr. Beausoleil. Today are the final cuts."

The custodian leaned on his broom as he watched me run across the court and put in a lay-up.

"You remind me of Larry Bird," he called. "He practiced shooting 500 free throws every day at 6:00 in the morning."

"No kidding? 500?"

Mr. Beausoleil nodded. "Practice and dedication is what made him the player he is today."

I smiled. Then I tried to concentrate. Mom said to establish a routine for shooting free throws. I bounced the ball three times, took one deep breath and bounced the ball again. Then I sank down on my knees and aimed.

The ball hit the back of the rim and fell in.

Swish!

I had my routine!

For the next 45 minutes I did nothing but shoot free throws using the same steps.

That was when Derrick arrived. "How many did you make?" he called from the back of the gym.

"About 75 percent."

Derrick checked his clipboard. "That's good! It might be the best on the team."

Then Derrick broke my concentration with his next comment. "The coach gave me two free tickets to the Thanksgiving Dance this Saturday night for helping him organize all the equipment. Guess who I'm asking?"

I stopped bouncing the ball. "Chloe?"

"Funny. You know who. The prettiest girl in seventh grade. Ellen Fairchild."

For the first time in 12 hours I wasn't thinking about basketball. I was thinking about how hurt

Derrick was going to be. "Why don't you ask someone else?"

"You're not serious."

"Well, girls can be funny. They change their minds a lot about things." I tried to prepare Derrick.

"Don't worry. Ellen is hoping I'll ask her. Just yesterday she said she wanted to go with someone special. And you and I know who that special guy is, right?"

I took a deep breath like I did before a free throw. This was not an easy shot. "Yeah, I know."

"Why don't you ask someone?" Derrick suggested.

"Nah. I want to save my money."

"Good idea. What are you saving it for?"

I knew Derrick would understand. He was a banker at heart. But I didn't feel like telling him the reason.

"You're not wasting it on a stamp for that pen pal of yours?"

"Maybe."

"Stamps cost big bucks! They've gone up another three cents!"

I knew it. Buying a stamp was a major expenditure for Derrick. He was without a doubt the biggest tightwad I knew. The only reason he was planning to take Ellen to the dance was because he had free tickets.

"So, Orp, you still write to Jennifer? What a lost cause. She's a thousand miles away." Then he whispered, "You can't get a kiss in a letter."

That was when I jabbed him one. Ever since he got his first kiss with Ellen at the pet shop, he'd been bugging me about my getting mine.

"I'm not ready for stuff like that," I said. "I have to get to know her better. I don't even know what she thinks the sunrise looks like."

"I'll tell you what it looks like. A gold piece."

Derrick made it sound like there was just one answer.

When the bell rang, I got my stuff and went to class. It was hard to keep my mind on things today. I kept looking at the clock and wondering if I was going to make the A team.

CHAPTER SIX

Ellen Comes Courting; Chloe Calls Time Out

Every Friday morning I go to the Enrichment Resource Room. It's a neat place. You get to work on projects and study anything you want.

The resource room teacher, Mrs. Lewis, is really interesting. She's traveled all over Africa and Asia. Today she was wearing sphinx earrings and an elephant necklace.

"Well, Orp, now that your studies on George

Washington, Thomas Jefferson and Abraham Lincoln are finished, do you have an idea yet for a new project?"

"Not really. Although, I just discovered I love basketball."

"Splendid! It's a great sport. My brother played center when he was in school."

I was beginning to wonder who DIDN'T play basketball except Derrick.

"Could I do a project on basketball?" I asked.

"If it's educational, I don't see why not. Any ideas?"

"Well Mr. Beausoleil mentioned Larry Bird. I might like to study the lives of some basketball players and see if they had anything in common."

Mrs. Lewis clapped her hands. "Splendid. I think there would be a lot of interest in your findings!"

Then she added. "Bill Bradley was a pro player. He was a Rhodes scholar and is a senator. You might find his life very interesting."

She didn't have to say any more. I went to the library and checked out four biographies on sports stars: Larry Bird, Magic Johnson, Bill Bradley and Michael Jordan.

Just when I was getting into one of the books, Derrick came up to me. His eyes were red. He looked like he had been crying.

Oh no, I thought. Ellen told him.

I closed my book. "What happened?"

"She doesn't want to go to the dance with me. Can you believe it. Me . . . Derrick Jones turned down!"

I tried to console my pal. "Hey, don't feel bad. George Washington was turned down when he proposed to a girl. Look what he went on and did."

Derrick made a half smile. "True, he got his face on the dollar bill."

Most people would have said George Washington went on to become the "father of our country." Not Derrick.

Then he looked over at Ellen. "If I ever find out who the guy is that she does like, I'll . . . wring his neck!"

Suddenly I felt like a chicken. It was time to change the topic. Fast.

"Hey, Derrick, why don't you come over Saturday night and we can play a hot game of Monopoly?"

"Can I be banker?"

"You always are."

Just then Ellen started walking over to us.

"Excuse me," Derrick said. "I don't want her to see my red eyes."

He cut out for the bathroom.

I opened up my book to chapter two.

"Are you working on a project?"

I looked up. It was Ellen Fairchild. She smelled like soap, as usual, and her hair was tied back in two knotty pine barrettes. She was, without a doubt, the prettiest girl in seventh grade. "You really play basketball well, Orp. I was watching you shoot baskets yesterday."

"Really?" I was beginning to sweat under my armpits. Dealing with rejection is tough, but sometimes dealing with attention is tougher.

"I think you are going to be Cornell Middle School's new basketball star!"

I didn't feel comfortable about that prediction. Especially since I hadn't made the team yet.

"Well, I love playing the sport. I even dreamt about it last night."

"Really? Tell me about your dream," she said, sitting down next to me. This was getting dangerous. Derrick would be coming back any minute now.

When her leg touched mine, I knew I was in trouble. Quickly I spotted Chloe in the resource room. This was one time I was glad she was in the enrichment program.

She was watching some guy named Cleveland working on an electricity project. When she caught my eye she could tell I was signaling for help. My eyebrows were going up and down and my eyeballs were going sideways.

Chloe sent me an I-got-your-message-look and came over. "Hi, Ellen. Hi, Orp," she said.

Ellen smiled a little. She didn't seem real happy to have an interruption. "Weren't you helping Cleveland with his project on circuits?"

"Yes, but I need a break. It's time to bug my brother for a while."

Ellen made a face. Then she did something that I never expected. "Would you go to the Thanksgiving Dance with me, Orp—this Saturday?"

I was shocked! She actually asked me right in front of my sister. And in the same room with Derrick. He was back now and looking over at the three of us. He had this desperate, hurt look on his face.

I looked at Ellen's eyes. They reminded me of the center of Milky Way candy bars—caramel brown. They were so sweet.

"Would you?" Ellen asked again.

Chloe knew I was struggling. My whole body was frozen, and I couldn't get one word out.

"Sorry, Ellen," Chloe said. "He promised he would take me."

Ellen stood up. "You are taking your SISTER to the dance?"

It was a miracle. I had an out. "Well, she really wants to go, and Mom said I have to take her.

It's her first dance and all. So, I said I'd do it this once."

Ellen looked disappointed. "Well, I'll see you at the dance. Maybe I'll go stag."

I tried not to smile too much. I didn't want to lead her on.

After she left, I took a deep breath. What a close call!

"Thanks, Chloe," I said. "You really saved my life."

"Good." Then after she got up she said, "I think I'd like an orchid to go with my purple dress."

Suddenly the reality of the situation hit me. Yes, I got out of a desperate situation, saved my friendship with Derrick and saved Ellen from the embarrassment of my saying no. But . . . NOW, I was faced with actually taking my sister to a dance.

Just thinking about it made my head heavy. It dropped to the desk like a bowling ball.

Bonk!

CHAPTER SEVEN

Final Tryouts

At 3:00, Derrick and I walked to the gym.

"Want to quit basketball?" Derrick asked.

"Why?"

"Well, the reason I wanted to be a statistician was to see Ellen Fairchild. Now that she doesn't want to see me, I shouldn't be around her."

I stopped in front of the two glass gym doors. "Do you like doing stats?"

"Kind of, yes. I feel important. The coach relies on me for facts and figures. I'm good at it."

"Keep doing it then! I love basketball, Derrick. I plan to keep doing it as long as I can. We can share that seat on the team bus and have a good time going to all the games together . . . if I make the team."

Derrick pushed open the door. "You'll make it. I heard the custodian talking to the coach today. He told him you were in the gym practicing at 6:00."

"Did the coach say he was going to pick me?"

"He said you were a dedicated player."

I started bouncing the ball in the gym. "We'll celebrate if I make the team, okay?"

"Saturday night over our Monopoly game," Derrick replied.

I stopped bouncing the ball. Life seemed awfully complicated sometimes. "Eh . . . do you want to go stag with Chloe and me to the dance?"

"You're kidding? You're taking Chloe?"

"It's kind of a long story."

Derrick could tell by my long face. "I know. Having a sister isn't easy. I'm just glad mine is in college. I'll think about it, Orp."

Moses and Ike were shooting baskets when I got down to the hoop. Bill Brown was tying his sneakers, while Danny Chin had the basketball on his index finger and was spinning it.

"Wow!" I said. "How do you do that?" Dad or Mom didn't cover that skill.

"It's easy. Any basketball player can do it," Ike joined in. Then he spun the ball on his finger high above his head like Danny.

I decided to give it a try. I held up my right

36

arm, set the ball on my finger and whirled it. The basketball came tumbling down on my head.

And the guys cracked up.

I didn't like being laughed at. I could do some great things with a baseball, but they didn't know about that.

When the coach blew his whistle, we all took laps. Bill Brown ran next to me. "Did you practice your moves in the attic?"

"My mom had a fit about bouncing the ball on her ceiling, so I practiced out in the garage."

"Hey, that's great you've got outside lights."

"We do as long as it's the Christmas season."

Bill laughed.

After we ran three more laps, we lined up for lay-ups. Ike was the tallest guy on the team at six feet. He was the only one who could dunk the ball.

That was when I started to wonder how tall I might be. Dad was 6'1". Mom was 5'10". Uncle Gus—my mom's brother—was 6'3"! Maybe I would be as tall as George Washington— 6'2", or Thomas Jefferson— 6'2½", or Abe Lincoln— 6'4". Then I started picturing those presidents going in for lay-ups. I wondered if they would have been good basketball players. Ol' Abe could probably teach me how to do a slam dunk.

I stopped thinking about height when Bill tossed me the ball. I dribbled up the court and jumped high, putting a soft shot into the net.

Ike followed with a leap and a quick shot to the hoop from the right side of the basket. When the ball rolled around the rim several times before falling in, I said, "You shoot like my mother."

Ike gave me this dirty look.

"I wouldn't tell him that again," Moses whispered.

"It was meant as a compliment."

"Ike doesn't know that."

After we did some shooting, dribbling and passing, the coach had us shoot 20 free throws a piece.

Ike went first and made 16.

"Someone try to beat that!" he said, tossing the ball to Moses.

When it was finally my turn, no one had.

I dribbled the ball three times, took a breath, dribbled once and then sank down to shoot.

Swish. Danny Chin held up one finger.

Swish. Swish. Now he held up three.

When he got to eleven, Moses put his finger up and started counting.

Swish. Twelve.

When I finally missed two, Ike smiled a little.

Three minutes later, I made 15 free throws with two turns left. Bill Brown gave me the A-okay sign.

Ike looked worried.

The next two free throws had to be perfect if I

was going to beat Ike's record. Carefully I did my same routine. Dribbled the ball three times, took a breath, dribbled once more and then sank down to shoot.

Swish! Moses was holding up six fingers now. Danny kept holding up ten.

Ike covered his eyes. He didn't want to watch my last free throw. I sure did. It rolled around the rim twice before it fell in.

Seventeen!

"Where did you learn to shoot free throws like that?" Ike asked.

"From my mother. She was captain of her bas-ketball team."

"No kidding? So you weren't just putting me down."

"No. I was giving you a compliment."

Ike took a step toward me. "Well, I'm giving you one. You're a good free-throw shooter."

"It takes one to know one," Moses added.

Ike slapped Moses five. Then he turned around and faced me. His hand was outstretched.

I slapped it.

I'll remember that first five with Ike. It was the beginning of our team spirit.

At the end of the tryouts, the coach had us gather round. I noticed the cheerleaders were watching from the bleachers. Derrick had his eyes on the team. I knew he wouldn't want eye contact with Ellen.

"One great thing about basketball at Cornell Middle School," the coach said, "is that everyone makes the team. We have two teams at Cornell. An A team and a B team. When I read your name, you'll know which one you're on."

"Ike Farley, Moses Miller, Danny Chin, Bill Brown . . ."

Everyone knew Coach Casey was starting with the A team.

When he got to the 12th player, I was beginning to get nervous. "This last guy is going to be a real spark for the A team. He's dedicated and loves the game. Orville Rudemeyer Pygenski."

Everyone looked around. They didn't know who that was. Ike spoke up, "Orp didn't make it?"

"THAT'S ME!" I shouted.

I jumped in the air and gave Ike a high five so hard, it stung my hand. Then Moses, Bill and Danny came over and slapped me five. It was a great feeling!

When Derrick and I rode our bikes home that night, he joked, "We can always celebrate your making the A team by taking turns dancing with your sister Saturday night."

"That's NOT funny," I grumbled. "If I do any dancing on that gym floor, it will be with a basketball."

CHAPTER EIGHT

Saturday Visitors

Saturday morning, I got up at sunrise with the chirping birds and worked on my 200 free throws in the driveway. Dad came out in a coat over his bathrobe at 7:00. He was holding a cup of steaming coffee.

"How many did you put in?"

"175."

"Well, I can see you are your mother's son."

I smiled.

"Our first game is Thanksgiving Day."

"Thanksgiving?"

"At 7:00."

"I'll tell your mother to put the turkey on in the morning."

"Hope it fits her," I said.

Dad laughed. "You've been talking to your Uncle Gus!"

"Yup! I called him last night at the gas station and told him I made the A team. He's stopping by today and is going to show me a few things. I didn't know he was an All-American in community college."

Dad watched me make a five-foot jumper. "Your Uncle Gus was amazing. He had this hook shot that no one could block. His team won everything that year. I thought he might go on and finish at a four-year school, but he broke his ankle real bad and never got into shape again. That's when he decided to open up his own gas station."

"Gus Stasion's Gas Station," I said as I shot a lay-up. What a weirdo. Names were unique in my family.

"Well, son, I'm going back in. It's chilly out here. I'm glad you put on your orange earmuffs. You warm enough in that jacket? We're supposed to get snow flurries today."

"Plenty warm," I said, snapping all my buttons.

"Anything you want me to pick up for you today? Need some tennis shoes or something?"

I stopped and thought about it. "Yeah, there is something."

"What is it, Orvie?"

42

"An orchid. I'm going to the school dance tonight."

"Well, you really are coming up in the world. First the basketball team, now a date! Who's the lucky girl? Anyone I know?"

"Yeah. Chloe."

"WHAT?"

"It's a long story, Dad. I just promised I'd take her. It's her first dance. I can look out for her."

"One orchid coming up," Dad said, laughing.

"I'M NOT DANCING WITH HER!" I called as he went back into the house. I figured I could drink punch and finish my Bill Bradley book.

That afternoon, Uncle Gus arrived in his truck. I could hear him coming down the street. His muffler had fallen off. He never gets around to doing repairs on his own machines.

When he hopped out of the truck, he had a green basketball with him. As he bounced it up the driveway, he pretended he was a radio announcer. "And Gus Stasion steals the ball, dribbles, jumps, shoots . . ."

Swish!

"The crowd cheers!" Uncle Gus continued. "It's the winning shot!"

I couldn't believe it. That thing was the longest three-pointer I ever saw! "Gee, Uncle Gus, you're an All-American!"

"Was." Then he patted his right foot. "The old body just couldn't keep up."

"Could you teach me how to make a hook shot?"

"Sure, partner. It's a good one to learn. The hook shot is very difficult to defend against. First of all, have your back to the free-throw lane. Take a step with your left foot toward the basket like this and . . ."

Swish!

I tried it.

The ball hit the garage roof and bounced back.

"You'll get it. You just have to work on it."

We shot baskets for 45 minutes. It was a great workout. I felt like I was playing with a Boston Celtic player. No doubt about it. Basketball was in my family tree.

"Hear you have a hot date tonight," Gus said, going in for a slam dunk.

"Funny," I said, catching his chest pass. I jumped and swished one from five feet out. That was beginning to be my favorite shot. "How did you find out?"

"Chloe asked if I would be your chauffeur."

"She thinks of everything. So, are you?"

"Why not? Trang and I have nothing better to do."

I liked Trang Foo. That was Uncle Gus's new girlfriend. They were a perfect match. She liked corny jokes and was good at sports. Every time we played whiffle ball in the backyard, she knocked it over the clothesline. She also had a mind of her own. She kept Gus guessing what she would do next. I was thinking maybe the next time we had a family outing we could all play basketball.

When Gus had to leave, he said, "Pick you up at 7:00?"

That was when I remembered Jenny Lee.

"Make that 7:15. I have to make a long distance phone call at 7:00."

"So, you have a COUPLE of girlfriends, Orp."

That did it! I took the basketball and arced a shot right at him.

"OUCH!" Uncle Gus exclaimed, rubbing his buns.

My hook shot was definitely improving.

CHAPTER NINE

Talking Long Distance

I looked up Jenny Lee's phone number in my address book. Then I stared at the kitchen phone for about ten minutes. This wasn't easy. I hadn't talked to Jenny Lee for four months.

Suddenly someone banged on the back door.

I opened it and saw it was Derrick. "I decided not to let a free ticket go to waste. I was going to give you the other one, but I had a chance to sell it to a guy on the B team."

That figured. I didn't know when Derrick ever treated me to anything.

"What do you think?" Derrick said, straightening his tie. "The girls will be overcome by my handsome looks?"

"Maybe," I said. "Where did you get those socks?"

Derrick lifted his pant legs. They were red with green dollar signs. "My sister, Dora, sent them to me from college."

We both laughed. "Guess Dora knows you are interested in money."

"I told her when I'm thirty I'm going to be president of a bank, and I'll know how much money my bank has to the penny."

That gave me an idea. I didn't want Derrick hanging around while I made my private call. "Hey, want to do me a favor?"

"What?"

"Take my Monopoly set, count the money and tell me if it's all there." Derrick was probably the only guy around who knew how much money was supposed to be in each set: $15,140.

"Sure. I'll work out here in the dining room."

I took the phone into the bathroom. I needed privacy. I closed the door and looked up Jenny Lee's phone number again in my address book. Then I started dialing. There was no time to be nervous now. I had to do it.

Listening to the phone ringing on the other end made my stomach turn. I felt like I was asking Jenny Lee for a date or something.

47

"Hello?" someone said after the third ring.

"Mr. Washburn?"

"Yes."

"Hi! This is Orville Pygenski calling from Connecticut. Is Jenny Lee there?"

"She'll be here in a moment. How are you? Keeping warm? Hope your heating system in the winter is better than your cooling system in the summer."

I laughed. Dad wouldn't appreciate Melvin Washburn's comment. He didn't appreciate Melvin's comments when he was here visiting. He complained a lot about our fan not working in the middle of July. And then when it was working he complained about it being so loud.

"How are your parents?"

"Fine."

"Your dad buy a new air conditioner yet?"

"No."

"Fix the TV knob?"

Just when I started to say no, I heard this voice in the background saying, "Dad!"

"Here she is," Mr. Washburn replied.

"Hello, Orville?"

It was her. And her voice was so sweet and calm.

"Hi, Jenny Lee. What are you doing?"

"Right now?"

"Right now."

"My favorite thing."

"What's that?"

"Talking to you."

I sank down in the tub and stared at my two big toes. They were curling up.

"Orville? Are you still there?"

I wasn't sure. It seemed like heaven to me. I suddenly felt airborne. "So how is your astronomy?"

"Good. I got two books at the library today. Should I bring up the subject of basketball?"

"Yes! I made the A team."

"I'm so happy, Orville! You'll have to write me about your games. Do you have a favorite shot?"

"Free throws and a five-foot jumper."

Then I thought of something else. "When I am practicing my shooting in the morning, I get to see the sun come up."

"You do?"

"Does the sunrise remind you of something?"

"What a neat question, Orville. I'll have to think for a moment."

After a few seconds she said, "Once when I was sleeping outside, I watched the sunrise. It reminded me of . . . you won't laugh will you?"

"No."

"Well, it reminded me of an egg yolk. How about you, Orville?"

"A golden basketball."

"I love it!" Jenny Lee said.

"I like yours, too." It was hard to believe we were 1000 miles away. I felt so close to her.

"I'll call you, Orville, Thanksgiving evening. It's my turn."

"Great! My first game is then. I'll tell you if I got a chance to play much."

"Thanks for calling, Orville."

Every time she said my name, my toes curled up a little more. " 'Bye, Jenny Lee," I said, then put the phone back in the kitchen.

When I got to my room, I lay on my bed and just thought about things.

My mellow mood was shattered when Derrick barged in. "You've got problems, Orp. You're short one yellow ten, one blue fifty, and one green twenty. That's eighty bucks."

I stood up and tried to look concerned. "Really?"

"Really. You just have $15,060 dollars in your Monopoly set. And two minutes to get ready."

"Huh?" I looked at the clock.

It was 7:13. Uncle Gus was knocking on the door and hollering, "YOUR CHAUFFEUR IS HERE, AND A LOVELY LADY WITH AN ORCHID IS WAITING."

I closed my eyes. Why couldn't it have been Jenny Lee?

CHAPTER TEN

Limo-nade

"I'LL BE THERE IN A MINUTE!" I hollered back. I grabbed a striped tie, a white shirt and ran a comb through my hair once.

When we finally opened the door, we weren't prepared for what we saw.

Chloe was all dressed up.

Her hair was curly and bounced on her shoulders. Her purple dress was simple, but pretty. The orchid was in her hand. "You're my escort. You need to pin this on."

I buttoned my sports jacket and followed my sister into the living room. "You don't look half bad, Chloe."

"Thanks, Orp. Just don't stab me to death."

"You look like someone who has big bucks in the bank, Chloe," Derrick added.

Chloe made a face. "Orville Redenbacher, the guy who makes popcorn, has money in the bank. Do I look like him?" She didn't care for the compliment.

"Ouch!" I said. "I just stabbed myself."

Dad laughed. "You have my sympathy. My fingers are still sore from hammer wounds."

"There," I said, stepping back. "I did it."

When Chloe turned to look at the mirror on the closet, the corsage fell off and landed on the floor in front of Ralph. He pawed at it like it was a hand grenade.

Suddenly there was a big booming sound.

"Stand back!" I said. "That corsage is loaded."

Uncle Gus was the only one who cracked up. He likes dumb jokes.

"It's just a little thunder," Chloe replied.

"I'll put it on you," Trang said. We all watched her do it. Her fingernails were painted with gold polish and red suns. They reminded me of the sunrise and Jenny Lee. I sure wished I was taking her to the dance instead of Chloe.

Uncle Gus pulled out a beret and put it on his head. "Everyone ready for our chariot?"

I laughed. Here we were all dressed up and getting into the Bomb Machine that needed a muffler.

Mom was taking pictures with her Kodak. "You two boys stand next to Chloe and smile."

Click.

"Now Uncle Gus and Trang you stand next to each other."

Click.

"All five of you stand close together and smile."

Click. My dad got up and grabbed Mom. "Take a picture of us, Gus."

"Oh no!" Mom objected. "My hair isn't combed. I'm wearing this silly apron. No . . ."

Click. Click.

"Shall we go?" Chloe said, looking at the clock on the mantle. "This Cinderella turns into a pumpkin at 9:30. Now it's 7:30! We'll be the last to arrive."

"Late is fashionable," Derrick said. Then he added, "Dora said that once when she was going to her high school prom."

Chloe took her notebook with her. "Just in case I get any ideas for a new plot."

That reminded me, I needed my Bill Bradley book. I picked it up and put it under my arm.

Derrick made a face. "Are we going to the library or a dance?"

Uncle Gus laughed. "I'll warm up the chariot."

"Have a wonderful time!" Mom said, hugging Chloe and then me. "Now share this big umbrella. You don't want to get wet."

This was getting to be too big a deal.

As soon as we stepped outside in the drizzling rain, we were shocked. The truck with no muffler was not parked out in front. Instead, there was a limousine!

"What is *that*?" I asked.

"*Whose* is that?" My dad asked.

"How *much* did that baby cost?" Derrick said.

Trang smiled. "Daddy let me borrow it. It belongs to the Fu Chow Company."

"You own a company?" Derrick asked.

"Yes. It's a soy sauce company. We also make chop suey vegetables."

"Wow!" he said, getting into the car. Chloe got in next. As soon as I sat down I tested the controls. I pushed the window buttons and got sprayed in the face with rain. They worked. I pushed a few other buttons. One turned on the radio, the other opened a cabinet. Inside were soda and glasses.

"Help yourself to the limo-nade," Trang said from the front of the car.

We all cracked up.

Uncle Gus drove the limo down the street. "I don't drink and drive."

Trang patted Gus on the shoulder. "How about you three in the backseat?"

"No thanks," Chloe said. "I might spill some on

my dress. Who knows. Cleveland might be there tonight."

"Who's Cleveland?" Derrick asked, taking a glass of limo-nade.

"He's the guy that's in our Enrichment Room on Friday mornings. The other fifth grader. He's working on a project in electricity."

"Oh, yeah. He's tall with glasses and wears those baggy plaid pants."

"That's him," Chloe said with a sigh. "But he never notices me. Well, once he did."

"Really?" Derrick was curious. "When was that?" he asked, filling another glass.

"He asked me if I had a double A battery."

"Did you?" I was mildly curious.

"No, but I do tonight," and she opened her purse. Inside were four batteries in all different sizes, and a pen flashlight.

I shook my head. Chloe was resourceful. And tonight she was pretty. Maybe after writing so many novels, she would have a romantic story of her own to write.

When the limo pulled up in front of the gym, Uncle Gus started howling like a dog, "Singing in the rain, just singing in the rain, what a glorious feeling, I'm happy again!"

Uncle Gus's singing was as bad as his jokes. I was glad my friends couldn't hear him.

A lot of the kids in the gym lobby were looking

out the glass doors. I saw Moses with his girl-friend. Bill Brown and Ike Farley were standing together. Ellen Fairchild was huddling with some cheerleaders. Everyone was watching us.

"See you at 9:30," Uncle Gus said, tipping his cap.

"What will you guys do for two hours?" I asked.

"We'll go cruising," Uncle Gus said, pulling his beret down on his forehead.

I knew they would have a good time.

Derrick stepped out and opened the big black umbrella. Then he offered Chloe his arm. "We might as well make a good entrance."

I decided not to join them. I didn't mind getting a little wet, but I did want to protect Bill Bradley, so I stuffed the book inside my jacket.

As the three of us walked up the gym steps, a crowd of people gathered at the door to watch. Uncle Gus didn't disappoint them. He took a wide turn through a puddle, made a big splash, and showed off the license plate, FU CHOW 1.

It was showtime all right.

The beginning of a disaster movie!

CHAPTER ELEVEN

A Real Disaster

As soon as we pushed open the doors, Moses and Ike came over. "We didn't know you were rich, Orp," Moses said.

"I'm not," I laughed. "The limo belongs to a friend."

"How's the dance?" Derrick asked.

"The teachers' band isn't half bad, but no one is dancing yet," Ike said.

"Good," Derrick replied. "I can start things off. But first, I have to use the room." Then he whispered to me, "Three glasses of limo-nade is hard on the kidneys."

As Derrick raced off, I looked around the gym. Cleveland was eating potato chips at the refreshment table. All I had to do was get Chloe and Mr. Electricity together and I would be free from this dance disaster. I motioned to Cleveland to come over.

Then I spotted Ellen by the big papier mâché turkey. She was smiling and waving and walking toward me! Her yellow dress rustled as she came closer. When she was right in front of me, I could smell her soapy skin and see her pearl barrettes. They were in the shape of crescent moons.

"Hi, Orp."

"Hi, Ellen."

Ellen gave my sister a quick hello.

"Want to start things off, Orp?" Ellen asked.

"Me?" I raised my eyebrows. I had to stall the situation. I couldn't dance with her. Derrick would be crushed.

"Let's go," she said, slipping her hand in mine. Now I could smell her gardenia perfume. Getting out of this was going to be tricky.

Suddenly a crack of thunder hit the gym. Everyone stared at the lightning flashing in through the windows. I seized the opportunity to break away from Ellen. "Look at that streak!" I shouted.

"You want to see me?" Cleveland interrupted.

What timing!

Quickly I whispered in Cleveland's ear. "Tag in on me in thirty seconds. I won't last much longer.

"Ellen," I said, "I promised my sister the first dance."

Chloe beamed.

Ellen looked shocked. Then when I saw Derrick coming over, I decided to do some matchmaking. "You know, Ellen. Derrick told me he thought you had the most beautiful eyes at Cornell School. He said they reminded him of the center of Milky Way candy bars."

"Really? Usually Derrick says I look like someone who has big bucks in the bank. It's not very romantic. But caramel brown eyes ... ooooh that's sweet."

Chloe started to cough and choke as I led her out to the middle of the gym floor. "That was pretty bad, Orp," she mumbled.

But it worked. Derrick and Ellen were walking out to the dance floor together. As we waited for the music to start, I noticed a crowd of people moving around the sides of the gym to watch.

Then the band began playing. Mr. Ortega, the school baseball coach was blowing on his trumpet. The other five teachers joined in with their instruments. It was a slow tune. This was going to be painful. I checked my watch then put my arm around Chloe's waist and held her other hand. I tried to move my feet to the beat of the music but it was hard. I never took dancing lessons.

How long could 30 seconds be?

Cleveland was staring at his watch. I picked the right guy. A scientist.

"Slide your feet back and forth," Chloe whispered.

Just as I tried to concentrate on moving my feet, I heard this familiar English accent calling to me.

I looked up. It was Mrs. Lewis.

She was at the dance with a home video camera!

"Orp, you look splendid with Chloe. Smile! We're going to show this at the school assembly, just as soon as I find the 'on' switch."

I panicked. How could I ever live through this? Dancing with my sister was one thing. Having the event recorded in video history was another. NEVER! I looked at my watch. Ten seconds to go. Cleveland was going to be my lifesaver.

"You are a horrible dancer!" Chloe complained as she pulled back. "Don't bother asking me again. That's the second time you've stepped on my foot."

Ahhhhhhh, I thought. My ticket to freedom. Cleveland was on his way over to tag in!

"They make these machines so complicated," Mrs. Lewis grumbled. "Cleveland! You're just the one I need. Please show me where the 'on' switch is."

I was dying. This wasn't supposed to happen. Who could save me now?

I gave Derrick a pleeeeeese-save-me-look, but he was having too much fun to notice. He was dancing a waltz with Ellen and spinning her around and dipping her back. Some people started applauding. I had no idea he was such a good dancer.

"It's on!" Mrs. Lewis exclaimed. "Ready action, kids! Now, Cleveland, you stay with me, while I run the first five minutes of tape."

Cleveland looked over at me and shrugged.

I gave him my most desperate, begging look but it didn't do any good.

Just as Mrs. Lewis was videotaping Derrick and Ellen doing a double twirl, a miracle happened.

A bolt of thunder cracked and the lights went out. Everyone started screaming. Chloe flicked on her pen flashlight and ran off. I was standing there in the dark. Alone.

It was a miracle.

Thank you, God.

Mr. Ortega shouted for everyone to remain calm. Mrs. Lewis didn't hear him. She was calling for Cleveland. "Where's the 'off' button? I'm wasting film and money."

"Money? Where?" It was Derrick's voice.

Ellen was laughing.

"Everyone sit down and be calm!" Mr. Ortega shouted. "We don't want anyone to trip."

Just then the refreshment table came crashing to the floor. When the lights came back on, Moses was sitting in the punch bowl with his girlfriend on his lap. People were stepping on the open-faced tuna sandwiches and smashing potato chips.

"I'll take care of it," Mr. Beausoleil said as he whipped out a mop, broom and dust pan.

While most of the students tried to help the janitor clean up, I noticed Chloe and Cleveland were talking to each other.

"Next time I'll pack fuses in my purse, not batteries," Chloe said.

"We helped the janitor check the circuit breaker, thanks to your handy flashlight. Good thing we know a lot about circuits, right, Chloe?"

"Right, Cleveland." Then they took a step toward each other and held hands. It looked like they were making their own electricity. I could see sparks in their eyes.

When I looked for Derrick and Ellen, I found them behind the papier mâché turkey. They were enjoying their second kiss.

Or was it the third?

I pulled out a chair next to the mural of the Mayflower and started reading my Bill Bradley book. Five minutes later, Coach Casey came over. I didn't even realize he was there.

"Well, everything seems to be back to normal. We got another punch bowl and more sandwiches from the cafeteria. The floor is just about dry. So is Moses. I gave him some sweatpants from the gym locker to change into. Planning to dance again?"

"I better not inflict any more casualties," I said. "I'm deadly on the dance floor."

The coach laughed. "Apparently you're deadly on the baseball diamond too. I was talking to Mr. Ortega. He told me about your fastball that's right on target. I didn't know I had an all-star pitcher on our basketball team."

I tried to be modest, so I shrugged. "Well, that's because he saw me play in Little League. This is my first year to play for a school team. I'm going to have to work hard like Bill Bradley did." I held up my book. "Did you know he practiced every day of the year for three hours?"

"Bradley was one of the best. Maybe you'll be one of the best too, Orp."

I gave the coach a big smile. His comment made me feel good. I thought this dance was going to be a real disaster, but Derrick, Chloe and I survived pretty well.

CHAPTER TWELVE

Time for the Thanksgiving Bird

Thanksgiving Day it was snowing.

But I went out in the driveway anyway and shoveled out a court. Then I started my morning free throws.

Like Larry Bird.

My orange earmuffs helped. I wasn't cold. I was moving around too much.

After I hit 180 out of 200 free throws, I went back in the house. Mom and Dad were yelling at each other in the kitchen.

"Take a stitch over here but don't poke me with that needle again," Mom said.

"Hold the leg. It's slipping," Dad said.

I decided to leave the Thanksgiving bird to my parents. I went into the living room, where Chloe was watching the Macy's parade on TV.

"You're not working on a romance novel about the dance Saturday night?"

Chloe held up a diary. "Actually, I'm changing my mode. I like writing about what *I* am doing. I already put in Saturday night's activity. I just have to wait and see what happens today."

"Well, the Macy's parade should be an exciting entry," I joked.

Chloe gave me a look. "I'm going to your first basketball game tonight."

"You are?"

"Cleveland is going too."

"I hope I get some playing time. We're playing Hartford Catholic. They're not in our league, but it should be a good practice game."

"Hartford Catholic? They went to the state finals last year. You guys will be murdered, creamed, obliterated, axed, massacred . . ."

"You sound like an ad for a violent movie."

"It's the writer in me," Chloe explained. "Oh, by the way, Cleveland said he had a plan for lighting up our driveway."

"No kidding? Mr. Electricity strikes again!" I laughed. "Tell ol' Cleve I said thank you."

Chloe got up and turned the TV down with the needlenose pliers.

"Hey," I said, "do you think Cleveland could fix our TV knob?"

"I'll ask him. He's coming by after dinner."

At 3:00 P.M., everyone sat down to Thanksgiving dinner. Uncle Gus was there with Trang Foo, Mom, Dad, Chloe and me. Ralph positioned himself under the table and waited for some handouts.

Everything smelled so good—the turkey, sweet potatoes, mashed potatoes, green beans, stuffing, cranberries, pumpkin pie and whipped cream.

After Dad said the blessing, I started passing the food around. I decided not to take huge portions this year, since I had a game coming up.

"Did you play basketball in high school?" I asked Trang.

"I was a point guard."

Uncle Gus patted her on the back. "She was feared by all the other teams. There was no stopping her when she drove to the basket."

I laughed. Then I had to ask, but I decided to whisper the question. "How did you play with your long fingernails?"

"They're artificial," Uncle Gus boomed. "She can take them off whenever she wants to."

My mother gave her brother a look.

I gave the clock a look. I couldn't wait to get to the gym for our first game.

CHAPTER THIRTEEN

Orp the Brave?

"Who's going in whose car?" Dad asked as we all met outside the house.

"My chariot awaits!" Uncle Gus replied.

Chloe and Cleveland climbed in Mom and Dad's car. They're not dumb. I would have too, but sitting next to those two scientists wasn't my idea of a good time.

"I'll go with Uncle Gus," I shouted.

"Good," Trang answered. "He likes company. Now I can go in a car that doesn't sound like a cement truck." And she got in the backseat next to Chloe. Chloe moved closer to Cleveland. She seemed happy about that.

"You're not going with me?" Gus shouted.

Trang waved. "See you there."

I knew she had a mind of her own.

Gus gave me a look. "Well, hop in, partner. We'll be the first ones there. Do you have the map?"

I took out the print-out Coach Casey gave the team. Hartford Catholic was close to exit 31 on the South ramp. It was about 20 minutes away.

When Uncle Gus turned on the engine, I understood why Trang Foo preferred a normal car. This machine did a job on my eardrums. I took out my orange earmuffs from my duffel bag and put them on.

"Do you think we're driving to Alaska?" Gus asked.

I could barely hear my uncle. I just nodded.

Uncle Gus started humming the music from *Hoosiers* when we got to the highway. Then he recited his favorite lines, "There's more to the game than shooting. There's fundamentals and defense. Let's be real clear about what we're after here. Team, team, team. Five players on the floor functioning as one single unit. No one more important than the other. I love you guys."

That was when the truck started to sputter.

I looked at the gas tank. It was full. "WHAT'S THE PROBLEM?" I asked.

Uncle Gus kept pumping the accelerator. "Sounds like the engine is giving out."

68

I watched Uncle Gus steer the truck down the next exit. It was 23. When we got to the stop sign, the truck died.

"That's great!" I said. "I'm going to miss the warm-ups. Coach Casey is real strict about things like that. He won't let me play."

"Hang on to your earmuffs. You're talking to a mechanic." Uncle Gus got out of the truck, pushed it over to the side shoulder and took a look underneath. He took out a wrench, and some other tools, and did some work.

My basketball career was getting off to a great start! As I sat and fumed, Uncle Gus tinkered away. Finally, he jumped back in the cab and started the engine.

It revved up. "We're off!" After a few quick jerks, the truck lurched forward, popped two times and we got back on the highway.

"You'll be on time for the national anthem," Uncle Gus said.

Fifteen minutes later, we drove into the crowded parking lot of Hartford Catholic. Uncle Gus let me off by the door. I ran into the boys' gym and put on my uniform. Just as I ran out onto the floor, everyone was standing and singing "and the home of the brave."

"Brave . . ." I sang loudly, standing next to the coach and Moses. I wasn't feeling very brave when I saw Coach Casey's glaring look. "Missed the warm-ups, Orp. You'll have to do 100 sit-ups on your own. And then rest on the bench awhile."

"Yes, Coach," I said. Then I put my head down and stared at my sneakers.

What a way to start my first game.

On the bench.

CHAPTER FOURTEEN

Our First Game

I didn't expect there to be so many people at a game on Thanksgiving Day. Four bleachers were filled with fans. Derrick was going over his stats with the opposing coach. He was looking very important. Ellen was standing on two girls' shoulders and spelling C-O-R-N-E-L-L. Uncle Gus had his program rolled up and was hitting Trang on the head with it. He was probably punishing her for not riding with him in the truck.

Funny. I was being punished for riding *with* him. I did my 100 sit-ups. Now I was doing my sit-downs on the bench.

I noticed Chloe and Cleveland had notebooks. They probably wanted to keep their own statistics. Mom was clicking her camera, and Dad had pom poms! That was hard to picture.

"The starting line-ups . . ." a voice said from the microphone. "For Hartford Catholic . . ."

We watched the first five run out to the center of the floor. Two of them were taller than Ike. The Cornell fans were polite and applauded for the opposing team.

"And now starting for Cornell Middle School . . ."

Everyone in our rooting section stood up and cheered.

"Captain and center Ike Farley."

Ike ran out to the center of the floor and waited.

"Guards Moses Miller and Danny Chin."

More cheers. Danny ran out first and slapped Ike's hands, then Moses's hands.

"Forward Bill Brown and . . ."

After the fifth Cornell guy ran out, Ike shouted, "TOGETHER!"

The referee threw up a jump ball. The tall center from Hartford Catholic grabbed it and ran down the court to score a basket.

The game went back and forth the first two quarters. We led by two points, then they did. At halftime, the score was tied. We all ran into the boys' locker room.

"You're playing great!" Coach Casey said.

"Keep working the ball, keep hustling. We might just surprise a few people today."

Then he looked at me. "Think you'll be late to another game, Orp?"

"No, sir." Actually I was thankful we'd be riding the bus to our regular games.

"Orp, I'm starting you the second half," the coach said. "You're the fifth man."

I jumped to my feet. Those words, "I'm starting *you*" felt like three bolts of lightning shot through my body. I was energized—and ready!

Cornell had the ball at the opening of the second half. Danny passed it to Bill, and Bill dribbled it around the key. When he saw Moses open, he fired the ball to him. Moses took a jump shot but it bounced off the rim. I got the rebound and turned my back to the free-throw line. Holding the ball with both hands, I turned and hooked in a shot.

Everyone watched the ball make an arc to the basket. SWISH!

The rooting section jumped up and cheered. I could hear Uncle Gus's booming voice.

Cornell scored first.

Moses ran down the court with me. "Man, Kareem Abdul-Jabbar would like that one. You've got a sky-hook shot like he does!"

Ike gave me the thumbs-up sign.

The game continued to be close right up to the

73

final 40 seconds. Hartford Catholic was ahead by one point, 45-44. Coach Casey called a time out and told us to hold the ball; then take a shot the final few seconds.

Danny Chin worked the ball around the key. Bill Brown passed it back and forth to Danny. As the clock ticked away, it was 30 seconds, 20 seconds and then time to set up that final shot. Brown passed it to me. I saw Ike close to the basket so I threw it to him. Two opposing players boxed him in. He bounced it back to me. There wasn't much time left. I took my favorite shot, the five-foot jumper, and got slapped. The ball fell short of the basket, but I had two chances at the free-throw line with nine seconds to go.

Free throws.

I looked over and saw Mr. Beausoleil in the corner of the gym. He was wearing a Cornell cap. He held two fingers up for victory.

Just when I bounced the ball three times, the other coach called a time-out.

"They just want to ice the shooter," Coach Casey said. "They want you to think about your free-throw shooting and get cold."

Cold?

Where were my orange earmuffs? I was used to shooting in the cold. I took them out of my duffel bag and put them on.

When the referee blew his whistle, we walked

74

back to the line. I heard someone from Hartford Catholic say, "Who's the orange clown? He'll choke."

Routine.

I bounced the ball three times, took a deep breath and then bounced the ball again. Slowly I sank down on my knees and pushed the ball up with my right hand.

SWISH!

Everyone cheered. Ike came over and slapped me five. It was a tied ball game.

I positioned my feet again, making sure my left foot was a little ahead of my right. Then I began bouncing the ball three times.

Just when I was getting ready to aim, the opposing coach ran over to the referee. "This may just be a scrimmage game but, he can't wear any headgear."

The referee motioned for me to take off my earmuffs. I tossed them to the coach on the sidelines. Was this going to affect my next free-throw shot?

Whooooosh . . .

Everyone watched the ball hit the backboard, roll around the rim three times . . . and fall in.

I looked up at Mom. She was jumping up and down.

The cheerleaders did cartwheels. The rooting section roared. Mr. Beausoleil was waving his cap in the air.

Thanks, Mom, I thought.

Thanks, Dad.

Even, thanks, Uncle Gus. I couldn't have done this without you. Cornell Middle School was ahead by one point.

And then the cheering suddenly stopped.

Hartford Catholic inbounded the ball quickly to their big man who dribbled it down the court and took a ten-foot shot. Swish!

It went in. Now THEY were ahead by one point! Ike made a "T" with his hands, as our rooting section groaned.

"TIME OUT!" the referee shouted.

We all looked up. There was one second left on the game clock.

"All right, you guys," Coach Casey said. "Gather round. The game is not over yet."

We all looked at each other and frowned. How could we bring the ball all the way up the court, shoot and score in one second?

The coach detailed his plan. "We're going to inbound a long pass clear across the court. Ike is going to be standing five feet away from the basket on the right side. As soon as he catches the long pass, the clock starts ticking. So he shoots as soon as he gets the ball."

"Who can throw the ball that far and on target?" Moses complained.

"A baseball pitcher," Coach Casey said.

And then he looked at me. "Orp, this is your chance to use your all-star baseball skills. Ike needs a perfect throw. Can you do it?"

All the guys stared at me.

"I'll try my best," I said.

As we walked back down the court, I noticed the guys from Hartford Catholic were hugging each other. They thought the game was over and they had won.

Ike was standing five feet to the right side of the basket. Moses was at half court. Hartford Catholic had two guards on him. They thought I would throw the ball to him and he would fire a long bomb.

Danny and Billy were running back and forth to divert attention.

Finally the referee handed me the ball.

The crowd turned silent. Everything was still like my early mornings. The golden basketball was in my hands. I knew what I had to do. I could see Ike. He was open. As soon as the referee blew his whistle, I brought my right arm all the way back and then snapped it forward like I was delivering my fastball.

I tried to get it up so Ike would catch it in the air. WHOOOOOOOOOOSH! Everyone watched the ball travel across the court like a long range missile. All eyes were on the trajectory of the ball. Ike was ready and waiting. He reached for it in the air with both hands, pulling it down like a touchdown pass. As soon as his feet touched the ground he shot the ball.

The buzzer sounded. The game was over. Who won? I couldn't see!

Everyone was running around the court. Then there was a thunderous roar from the Cornell Middle School rooting section. I looked up at my dad. He was hugging Mom and they were jumping up and down.

Derrick flipped the scorecards. 47-46.

We won! Ike's shot was a bull's eye!

I galloped across the court. Coach Casey met me halfway and hugged me. I hugged him back. Then I jumped on Moses and Bill Brown and Danny Chin.

"We did it!" everyone shouted.

Then we picked up Ike and carried him around the court.

"I like that arm of yours," Ike shouted down at me.

"You made it count," I called back.

Ike jumped down and put his arms around us. "I love you guys."

As we headed for the locker room, I spotted my family again.

Click! Mom was there with her camera.

"This is the best game I've ever seen," Chloe

78

exclaimed. "I can't wait to write about it in my diary."

Dad came running down from the bleachers, waving those silly pom poms. "Didn't I tell you your baseball skills would come in handy?"

I gave Dad a big hug.

Uncle Gus hit me on the head with his program. "You know how to throw a round ball, kid!"

"I'm painting basketballs on my fingernails for the next game," Trang said.

I laughed. Boy, was I happy!

It seemed like I'd talked to everybody that night, except for Jenny Lee.

The best was for last.

CHAPTER FIFTEEN

Together

At 9:30 P.M. when we walked into the house, the phone was ringing and Ralph was barking.

I ran to the phone and nearly tripped over my dog. "Hello?"

"Orville?"

It was her sweet, calm voice.

"Jenny Lee, we won! I threw the basketball the length of the court, and Ike made a basket the last second of the game!"

"That's great! I'm so happy for you."

I took the cord and phone into the bathroom when I noticed everyone was coming into the kitchen for pumpkin pie.

After I closed the bathroom door and sat in the tub, I said, "Wish you could have seen the game."

"Me too. How were your free throws?"

"I made two important ones in the last nine seconds of the game."

"Thanks to your early-morning practices," she replied. "You know, Orville, you were so excited about basketball when we last talked, that I decided to try it myself."

"You did?" When I said that, a towel dropped on my head.

"I tried out for the girls' basketball team at our middle school here, and guess what?"

"What?" I positioned my feet on the faucet handles.

"The coach said I was a natural player. He has me playing guard. I love it too, Orville. Our first game is Saturday."

"Well, with your beautiful eyes, you'll be able to pass off to anyone."

I was surprised I said that. But I never could forget her blue eyes. Those two YMCA pools.

"Thanks, Orville."

"Well, when I come to Ohio, we can shoot a few baskets together."

"Together," she repeated.

I liked that.

"Happy Thanksgiving, Jenny Lee."

"Happy Thanksgiving to you, Orville. Did you give Ralph some pumpkin pie?"

She remembered my dog loves desserts.

"No. He throws up when he eats sweets."

She forgot that part.

Jenny Lee laughed. "Well, give him a hug for me."

"I will. It seems I've given everyone a hug tonight except . . . you."

That was when the phone went quiet and my toes curled up.

Somehow during that silence I felt like Jenny Lee and I were thinking the same thing. But neither of us could say it.

"I'll put that astronomy book in the mail tomorrow."

"Thanks, Orville. If I find any good autobiographies on basketball players, I'll send you some. After I read them first," she added.

I laughed. "Talk to you next week."

"Bye, Orville."

"Bye, Jenny Lee."

I sat in the tub for a minute just thinking about her, when Chloe barged in.

"You have to come outside and see the lighting Cleveland put in for you this afternoon."

That got me out of the tub quick.

Mom, Dad, Uncle Gus, Trang and Chloe watched as I switched on the lever next to the garage.

I couldn't believe it. There, in miniature white

Christmas lights, were the words, "ORP GOES TO THE HOOP."

"Let's play some round ball!" I shouted.

"Just for a few minutes. It's cold out here," Mom said, bouncing the ball in the driveway.

"Not me," Chloe said. "Someone has to be an individual around here. I don't care to play basketball, but I do care to write in my diary. Good night."

"Hey, Chloe," I said. "Are you going to write about the game?"

Chloe nodded.

"Maybe you'll read it back to me someday when we're older. This was probably the best night of my life."

Chloe raised her eyebrows. I think she was surprised that I wasn't making fun of her writing. "Sure. That's why I like keeping a diary. I can save the good times."

I gave my sister a smile. Then I ran back to the driveway. Dad passed Mom the ball, and she dribbled in for a basket.

Gus got the rebound and passed it to Trang.

"Oh no!" she said as some gold and red things went flying in the air.

"What's the matter?" we all asked.

"I forgot to take off my fingernails."

"Well, most of them are off now," Gus said.

Then we all just laughed, together.

83

Join in the Wild and Crazy Adventures with Some Trouble-Making Plants

by Nancy McArthur

THE PLANT THAT ATE DIRTY SOCKS

75493-2/$2.95 US/$3.50 Can

Michael's room was always a disaster area, strewn with all kinds of litter—heaps of paper and dirty socks everywhere. But that was before the appearance of the most amazing plants ever! Suddenly Michael's junk heap disappeared, eaten by two giant plants that gobbled up socks faster than anyone could supply them.

And Don't Miss

THE RETURN OF THE PLANT THAT ATE DIRTY SOCKS

75873-3/$2.95 US/$3.50 Can

It's vacation time and the sock eaters are going along with Michael and his family to Florida.

THE ESCAPE OF THE PLANT THAT ATE DIRTY SOCKS

76756-2/$3.50 US/$4.25 Can

Now that the sock-eating plants have learned to move themselves around, they're off on some wild adventures, with the whole family chasing after them.

Celebrating 40 Years of Cleary Kids!

CAMELOT presents
BEVERLY CLEARY FAVORITES!

☐ **HENRY HUGGINS**
70912-0 ($3.99 US/$4.99 Can)

☐ **HENRY AND BEEZUS**
70914-7 ($3.50 US/$4.25 Can)

☐ **HENRY AND THE CLUBHOUSE**
70915-5 ($3.99 US/$4.99 Can)

☐ **ELLEN TEBBITS**
70913-9 ($3.99 US/$4.99 Can)

☐ **HENRY AND RIBSY**
70917-1 ($3.99 US/$4.99 Can)

☐ **BEEZUS AND RAMONA**
70918-X ($3.99 US/$4.99 Can)

☐ **RAMONA AND HER FATHER**
70916-3 ($3.99 US/$4.99 Can)

☐ **MITCH AND AMY**
70925-2 ($3.50 US/$4.25 Can)

☐ **RUNAWAY RALPH**
70953-8 ($3.50 US/$4.25 Can)

☐ **RAMONA QUIMBY, AGE 8**
70956-2 ($3.99 US/$4.99 Can)

☐ **RIBSY**
70955-4 ($3.50 US/$4.25 Can)

☐ **STRIDER**
71236-9 ($3.99 US/$4.99 Can)

☐ **HENRY AND THE PAPER ROUTE**
70921-X ($3.50 US/$4.25 Can)

☐ **RAMONA AND HER MOTHER**
70952-X ($3.50 US/$4.25 Can)

☐ **OTIS SPOFFORD**
70919-8 ($3.50 US/$4.25 Can)

☐ **THE MOUSE AND THE MOTORCYCLE**
70924-4 ($3.99 US/$4.99 Can)

☐ **SOCKS**
70926-0 ($3.50 US/$4.25 Can)

☐ **EMILY'S RUNAWAY IMAGINATION**
70923-6 ($3.50 US/$4.25 Can)

☐ **MUGGIE MAGGIE**
71087-0 ($3.99 US/$4.99 Can)

☐ **RAMONA THE PEST**
70954-6 ($3.99 US/$4.99 Can)